The Second of the Fiskers Field Mouse Series

Dedicated to my
husband Tony with
my loving gratitude

"Influenza," Doctor Badger pronounced

Chapter 1

The exciting Journey

IT WAS WINTER, there was snow on the ground and Fiskers, the field mouse was not well. His throat was scratchy, his eyes ached and he felt very hot.

"Poor boy," said Fiskers' mother, "I am calling Dr. Badger."

Dr. Badger looked down Fiskers throat and took his temperature.

"Influenza," he pronounced. "Now young fellow, bed rest for you until you are well again." He handed Fiskers' mother a big bottle of Cherry flavoured

After a delicious spoonful of cough medicine, he fell fast asleep

cough medicine and after patting Fiskers' head, he left.

The little field mouse was feeling too ill to complain, so he changed into his pyjamas and climbed into bed. After a delicious spoonful of cherry cough medicine he fell fast asleep.

Three days later he began to feel so much better, but his mother said

"No Fiskers, Dr. Badger said one more day in bed."

Fiskers was bored now and missing school and all his woodland friends. He wondered what Reno Rabbit was doing after school and wished he could play with him.

The day was a long one for Fiskers, he read some old books again and practised a tune on his blue whistle which Santa had given him for

Fiskers loved Granny Gossamer

Christmas. He was feeling much happier when his mother came in with his hot milk drink and to kiss him goodnight. Fiskers was about to close his eyes when suddenly a dark shape filled his window. For a moment the little field mouse was startled, but when he saw it was Granny Gossamer, the biggest, oldest, spider in the wood, he couldn't stop smiling.

Fiskers loved Granny Gossamer. When he was just a toddler he became lost in the wood while he was out with his mother picking hazel nuts. Granny Gossamer found him and gently placing one of her eight hairy legs around him, she led him home safely to his frantic mother.

Granny had hundreds of grand-children and some of them were with

"Now Fiskers, just listen to this"

her now. They were helping her to carry a great big spider's web.

"Hello Granny Gossamer," said Fiskers beaming all over his little face. "How lovely to see you again."

Fiskers' mother had taught him to be very respectful and polite.
"Hello Fiskers" chorused all the grandchildren. "Just wait until we tell you your exciting news."

They scrambled over the window-sill after their Granny bringing the large cobweb with them.

"Now Fiskers just listen to this" said the large spider. "Santa Clause has a very good friend who lives at the North Pole, she is the Ice Queen and she has invited you to visit her at her Palace. She knows you have been ill and she also knows how bored you are and that

Crystal, the fairy, smiled and waved at Fiskers

you are now almost better. A Snow Goose is waiting outside with one of the Ice Queen's Light Fairies to take you to the North Pole now."

Fiskers eyes widened with wonder and delight at such a treat.

"You will be home for breakfast, so no harm will come to you, you lucky little field mouse," said Granny smiling at Fiskers. "Now, this cobweb cloak will keep you as warm as toast," and she and the little spiders all helped Fiskers to wrap the cloak snugly around him.

Sure enough there was a beautiful, large, white & black bird outside and on his neck the prettiest little fairy Fiskers had ever seen. She was wearing a green dress that floated around her and shimmered with a hundred lights in the moonlight. She smiled and waved at Fiskers.

How thrilling to feel the wind rushing past his whiskers

"My name is Crystal," she said, "Come and sit in front of me Fiskers, The Ice Queen is looking forward to meeting you, Santa has told us how kind you were to one of his little men, when you freed his beard from a bush in your wood. All the light fairies in the North Pole are longing to meet you too."

Fiskers felt a little shy at all the praise and attention he was getting. Granny Gossamer fussed around him and helped him to sit in front of the light fairy. She stroked his face and said "Goodbye Fiskers - you can tell us all about the North Pole and the Ice Queen's Palace tomorrow" and with those words the large Snow Goose flapped her wings and rose into the air with the sound of "Goodbyes" from all the little spiders.

Mother and Baby Beluga Whales

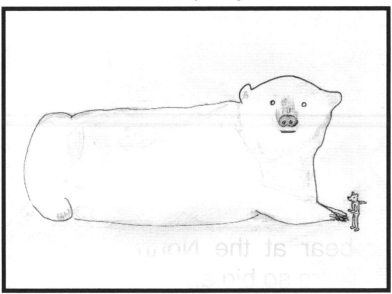

Polar Bears were so Big and he was so small!

CHAPTER 2

The Journey Begins

HOW THRILLING TO feel the wind rushing past his whiskers and seeing the ground beneath them turn so quickly to sea then the dark shadow of land on his right side.

"That is Norway," said Crystal. After more sea, Fiskers shouted, "Look Crystal there is a whale."

Crystal said, "Yes, and there is a baby whale swimming beside her. They are called Beluga Whales which are found in the Arctic Ocean."

Fiskers hoped he would not meet a polar bear at the North Pole. Polar bears were so big and he was so small.

There appeared on the horizon a magnificent Palace

with Towers reaching into the sky

The cobweb cloak kept the little mouse safe and warm. He felt sorry for the little light Fairy, who had nothing but her glowing, green dress, but was happy to see she did not appear to feel cold at all.

The fairy pointed to the snow laden ice below,

"This is the North Pole Fiskers and soon you will see the Ice Queen's Palace." The very next moment there appeared on the horizon, a magnificent Palace with towers reaching into the sky. Around it an aura of green, yellow and pink lights glowed.

When the Snow Goose landed on the ice, the huge, brown Palace doors opened and Fiskers was dazzled by the shower of light that floated swiftly towards them. As the light came closer, he could see it was coming from the

The doors were opening

dresses of many little fairies. There were some in green dresses, some in pink and some in yellow and they gathered around Fiskers excitedly stroking his whiskers, his ears and his tail. They were all talking at once until a trumpet sounded from inside the Palace.

"Come on," said the fairies, "The Ice Queen is calling you." Little Crystal took Fiskers' paw and led him through the Palace doors.

As he stepped inside, Fiskers had the biggest surprise. He saw that the doors were made of chocolate and the door handles were liquorice.

"How exciting," Fiskers said, "To have a Palace made of sweets."

Fiskers took a tiny corner piece from the edge of the door

"Yes, you can break a piece off, if you would like to taste some," said Crystal.

"Oh no," Fiskers was alarmed, "I wouldn't want to damage it." Crystal laughed.

"Just take a piece of chocolate and see what happens." Fiskers took a tiny corner piece from the edge of the door and he was amazed to see it grow back again immediately.

"How wonderful," he exclaimed and all the fairies laughed at his expression of astonishment.

"Come this way Fiskers." Crystal led him towards two big, green doors which opened automatically as they approached. Fiskers sniffed the delicious scent of peppermint and

Fiskers gasped at the breathtaking sight

realized that the doors were made of peppermint rock.

He saw a vast room beyond and Fiskers gasped at the breathtaking sight. The room had icicles hanging from the ceiling and each one was coloured in pastel shades of green, pink, yellow and blue. Little red lights covered all the walls and Fiskers thought the berries on them looked like his favourite scarlet dewdrop sweets he bought from Dame Wimple's shop in the wood back home. There was an arch made of blue ice crystals in several different shapes and they sparkled like diamonds over the head of the Ice Queen herself who was sitting on a throne of ice. Fiskers had never before seen such a breath-taking presence.

On her white, flowing hair was a crown of ice and her silver dress which

Welcome, welcome Fiskers to my Palace

flowed to the ground had a million little ice crystals twinkling away on it. Her feet were clad in what Fiskers thought were glass slippers but were really ice.

Fiskers felt a little nervous as he approached the throne, he had never spoken to Royalty before, but in a moment, the Ice Queen put him at ease by saying,

"Welcome, welcome Fiskers to my Palace, Santa speaks very highly of you. You are becoming quite a celebrity."

Fiskers replied, "Thank you your Majesty, I don't think I deserve it - I am just an ordinary field mouse."

"Ordinary!" Replied the Ice Queen, "Never, it would be a better world if others were as kind and considerate as you. Now my fairies have a treat for

Fiskers gasped at the wondrous sight

you. Come, we will go outside. They are going to perform a spectacle that can only be accomplished when conditions are right and that time is now."

With these words she clapped her hands and all the fairies rose into the air at once, flying high into the night sky and as they flew their dresses spread around them and Fiskers gasped at the wondrous shades of green and swirls of pink and yellow that cascaded across the sky as far as he could see. The Ice Queen smiled at his expression and said, "This is called the Aurora Borealis, Polar lights or Northern Lights. Those who have seen this may consider themselves privileged."

"I feel very privileged your Majesty," replied Fiskers, "Thank you so much for inviting me to your Palace at the Arctic to see the Northern Lights."

The Ice Queen giving Fiskers a scarlet dew drop

"Ah, a very polite and well brought up field mouse too," replied the Ice Queen.

The light fairies were beginning to land back on the ice and Fiskers could see the Snow Goose was positioning himself for the flight back to Fiskers' home.

"Just one minute little field mouse, I have a present for you." The Ice Queen reached up to a wall light and picked a red berry from one. "This will make your journey back home more pleasant," she said as she popped the red berry into Fiskers' mouth.

It **was** a scarlet dew drop and it **did** last the whole journey back to Fiskers' wood.

Fiskers' mummy wakes him up